P9-CAN-196

MAY 2 8 2009
JUN 0 9 2009
JAN

Romeo and Lou BLAST OFF

Derek Anderson

Simon & Schuster Books for Young Readers
New York London Toronto Sydney

TUNA
O
s

It was a perfectly delicious day to build something. The sun was golden, the air was sweet, and a blanket of fresh snow was waiting. So after breakfast Romeo and Lou hurried over to their favorite snowy, blowy hill.

They didn't know what to make, so they just started with one little snowball.
Romeo rolled.

And Lou pushed.

Romeo patted.

And Lou smooshed.
But it wasn't until they were
finished that they realized
what they'd made.

"What is it?" asked Lou.

"I think it's a rocket ship," said Romeo.

So they climbed aboard.

Lou didn't like to fly, but this rocket ship was just pretend.

They played in their new rocket ship all afternoon.

Then the stars came out. That's when one teeny shooting star streaked high above. The rocket ship let out a snowy sputter. And then an icy click.

"What was that?" asked Romeo as he felt a low rumble.

"I thought it was you," said Lou as he felt a large thump.

And suddenly they blasted off.
They looped and swirled over the snowy ground.
And twisted and twirled into the night.
Lou screamed the whole way.

The landing didn't go very well.
They skidded and bumped over hills and lumps until they rattled to a stop on a weird new world.

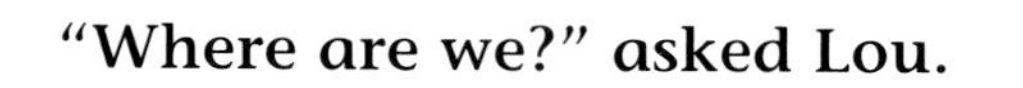

"Where are we?" asked Lou.

"I'm not sure," said Romeo. "But I think it's a different planet."

Lou looked at the rocket ship and whimpered. There wasn't much left of it.

"How are we going to get home?" asked Lou.

"I guess we'll have to find another way," said Romeo.

So Romeo and Lou went off to find another way home.

THE ONLY WAY
No DOGS ALLOWED
EXCEPT FRIDAYS
No PARKING EVER
PAY UP!
PARKING
$1 PER MINUTE
25¢
THE GOOD TIMES
UFO IN CITY
Are they here?

They soon got lost in a strange forest.

"Weird," said Romeo.

"These trees don't look anything like the ones back home," said Lou.

They were relieved when they saw another penguin and polar bear.

Romeo and Lou hurried over to ask for their help.

"Boy, are we glad to see you!" said Romeo and Lou.

But something wasn't right. The penguin was too big, and the polar bear was too small.

And they weren't helpful at all.

When Romeo asked for a rocket ride home, the big penguin said, "Well . . . who, uh . . . what?"

And the little polar bear didn't say anything. He just growled.

"Jeesh, what a grump," said Lou.

They tried to find someone else to help, but there weren't any other penguins or polar bears.

They spotted a seal, but he wouldn't even look at them.

"Is he spitting at us?" said Romeo.

"How rude," said Lou.

They even saw two walruses, but they were busy ice fishing.

"Don't they know that's not ice?" said Romeo.

"Silly walruses," said Lou.

Then they found what they were hoping for.
“A real live rocket ship!” said Romeo.
“We’re going home!” cried Lou.
Romeo and Lou quickly climbed aboard.

But before they could blast off, they were chased out
by a school of angry fish.

And then a shark showed up. Romeo and Lou ran.

The shark chased them down a bumpy hill
and over a long, rickety bridge.

Romeo and Lou ran for as long as they could, and when they didn't see the shark anymore, they found a place to hide. Romeo was still huffing and puffing when Lou began to sniffle.

"That was our last chance," cried Lou. "Now we're stuck here forever."

But Romeo was already thinking. "I know how to get home," he said.

"You do?" said Lou. "How?"

"The same way we got here. We have to build a rocket ship," said Romeo.

Lou liked that idea a lot, but there wasn't any snow. They would have to build it out of something else. And then Romeo spotted just the thing.

It wasn't perfect. They had to empty some things out. And it needed a little work.
So Romeo folded.

And Lou gnawed.

Romeo scrunched.

And Lou clawed.
And when it looked like a rocket ship,
they climbed aboard.

"Cross your toes," said Romeo.

"Please work," said Lou, even though he was still afraid to fly. "Please."

At first they didn't hear anything. There wasn't a snowy sputter. And there were no icy clicks. But soon they heard a low rumble. And a few large thumps.

And suddenly, to their surprise, the rocket ship took off.

"Hold on, you big fuzzball," said Romeo. "We're going home!"

"Oh, happy day!" cried Lou.

And as their rocket ship swished and swayed in the starry night, Romeo and Lou smiled all the way home.

For my pal, Friday, who inspired Lou's look and personality.

SIMON & SCHUSTER BOOKS FOR YOUNG READERS
An imprint of Simon & Schuster Children's Publishing Division
1230 Avenue of the Americas, New York, New York 10020

Book design by Daniel Roode
The text for this book is set in Stone Informal Semibold.
The illustrations for this book are rendered in acrylic paint.
Manufactured in China
2 4 6 8 10 9 7 5 3 1
Library of Congress Cataloging-in-Publication Data
Anderson, Derek, 1969–
Romeo and Lou blast off / written and illustrated by Derek Anderson.—1st ed.
p. cm.
Summary: When best friends Romeo and Lou, a penguin and a polar bear, build a rocket ship out of snow, it suddenly ignites and launches them on an adventure through the starry night.
ISBN-13: 978-1-4169-3784-5
ISBN-10: 1-4169-3784-6
[1. Rockets (Aeronautics)—Fiction. 2. Best friends—Fiction. 3. Friendship—Fiction. 4. Polar bear—Fiction. 5. Penguins—Fiction.]
I. Title.
PZ7.A53313Rom 2007
[E]—dc22
2006024822